W9-CIP-343

E   Muntean, Michaela   c.5
MU   Bicycle Bear Rides Again

GAYLORD MG

BICYCLE BEAR RIDES AGAIN

To librarians, parents, and teachers:

Bicycle Bear Rides Again is a Parents Magazine READ ALOUD Original — one title in a series of colorfully illustrated and fun-to-read stories that young readers will be sure to come back to time and time again.

Now, in this special school and library edition of *Bicycle Bear Rides Again*, adults have an even greater opportunity to increase children's responsiveness to reading and learning — and to have fun every step of the way.

When you finish this story, check the special section at the back of the book. There you will find games, projects, things to talk about, and other educational activities designed to make reading enjoyable by giving children and adults a chance to play together, work together, and talk over the story they have just read.

Bicycle Bear
Rides Again

by Michaela Muntean
pictures by Doug Cushman

Parents Magazine Press • *New York*

Gareth Stevens Publishing • Milwaukee

For a free color catalog describing Gareth Stevens' list of high-quality books, call 1-800-542-2595 (USA) or 1-800-461-9120 (Canada). Gareth Stevens' Fax: (414) 225-0377.

Parents Magazine READ ALOUD Originals:

A Garden for Miss Mouse
Aren't You Forgetting
    Something, Fiona?
Bicycle Bear
Bicycle Bear Rides Again
The Biggest Shadow in the Zoo
Bread and Honey
Buggly Bear's Hiccup Cure
But No Elephants
Cats! Cats! Cats!
The Cat's Pajamas
Clara Joins the Circus
The Clown-Arounds
The Clown-Arounds Go
    on Vacation
The Clown-Arounds Have
    a Party
Elephant Goes to School
The Fox with Cold Feet
Get Well, Clown-Arounds!
The Ghost in Dobbs Diner
The Giggle Book
The Goat Parade

Golly Gump Swallowed a Fly
Henry Babysits
Henry Goes West
Henry's Awful Mistake
Henry's Important Date
The Housekeeper's Dog
I'd Like to Be
The Little Witch Sisters
The Man Who Cooked
    for Himself
Milk and Cookies
Miss Mopp's Lucky Day
No Carrots for Harry!
Oh, So Silly!
The Old Man and the
    Afternoon Cat
One Little Monkey
The Peace-and-Quiet Diner
The Perfect Ride
Pets I Wouldn't Pick
Pickle Things
Pigs in the House
Rabbit's New Rug

Rupert, Polly, and Daisy
Sand Cake
Septimus Bean and His
    Amazing Machine
Sheldon's Lunch
Sherlock Chick and the
    Giant Egg Mystery
Sherlock Chick's First Case
The Silly Tail Book
Snow Lion
Socks for Supper
Sweet Dreams, Clown-Arounds!
Ten Furry Monsters
There's No Place Like Home
This Farm is a Mess
Those Terrible Toy-Breakers
Up Goes Mr. Downs
The Very Bumpy Bus Ride
Where's Rufus?
Who Put the Pepper in
    the Pot?
Witches Four

Library of Congress Cataloging-in-Publication Data

Muntean, Michaela.
    Bicycle Bear rides again / by Michaela Muntean ; pictures by Doug
Cushman. -- North American library ed.
        p. cm. -- (Parents magazine read aloud original)
    Summary: When his uncle Bicycle Bear takes a vacation, Trike Bear
attempts to take over his delivery job and finds it more difficult
than he had thought.
    ISBN 0-8368-0964-5
    [1. Bears--Fiction. 2. Delivery of goods--Fiction. 3. Bicycles
and bicycling--Fiction. 4. Uncles--Fiction. 5. Stories in rhyme.]
I. Cushman, Doug, ill. II. Title. III. Series.
[PZ8.3.M89Bk 1995]
[E]--dc20   93-15470

This North American library edition published in 1995 by Gareth Stevens Publishing, 1555 North RiverCenter Drive, Suite 201, Milwaukee, Wisconsin, 53212, USA, under an arrangement with Gruner + Jahr USA Publishing.

Printed in the United States of America

1 2 3 4 5 6 7 8 9 99 98 97 96 95

For Alexia, Paul,
and Colleen—M.M.

To Stephen—D.C.

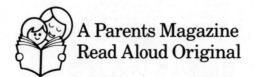A Parents Magazine
Read Aloud Original

"You can name any place,
Any place that you like—
I have been there and back
On the seat of a bike.

"From Peking to Paris,
From Sweden to Spain,
I have pedaled this world
Through snowstorms and rain."

"Through the darkest of nights,
Through the sun's strongest glare,
"I'm the one that you've called.
I am Bicycle Bear!

"I've delivered whatever
You've wanted to send
To your mother, your brother,
Your aunt, or a friend."

"But now winters seem longer.
(Are they getting colder?)
Or maybe it's just
That I'm getting older.

"There's a crick in my back.
There are creaks in my knees.
I would like to be warmed
By a tropical breeze."

"But who would take over?
Who would get the jobs done,
If I went away
To sit in the sun?"

He was puzzling and pedaling
Through that cold wintry air,
When along came his nephew,
Young Tricycle Bear.

Now Trike always asked
If he could help out,
For he dreamed that one day
He would have his own route.

"It's so good to see you!"
Said Bicycle Bear.
"For I was just thinking
Of going somewhere.

"But I would not feel right
About leaving town.
I'd worry that I'd let
My customers down."

"I'll take over," said Trike,
"While you get your rest.
If only you'd let me,
Why, I'd do my best!"

They quickly agreed,
Then set off for the station
So Bicycle Bear
Could start his vacation.

Trike went right to work,
But it really was rough.
The snow and the ice
Made delivering tough.

At the end of the day
He fell into his chair.
All the work he had done
Made him one tired bear.

The very next morning
Came a call from a mouse.
He wanted to know:
Could Trike move his house?

"No problem," said Trike,
"That should be a snap.
The house of a mouse
Could fit in my lap!"

If that had been true,
All would have been fine,
But that little mouse's family...

...Numbered ninety-nine!

The house had sixteen stories,
With two hundred and twenty rooms.
They were filled with cheese and chairs,
And blankets, beds, and brooms.

"I'm not sure how to do this.
But I'll *try*," said Tricycle Bear.
"The snow's too deep to pull this house.
Perhaps I'll float it through the air!"

So he went to get balloons.
He got four-hundred and four.
He tied them to the rooftop,
To the windows and the door.

"If this works," said Trike,
"This move will be a cinch."
But that house just would not budge.
No, it would not move an inch.

"Now what?" cried Trike.
"My life was going fine,
Until I met this family
That numbers ninety-nine!"

31

He sat down on his tricycle
To try and think things through.
He needed help to move this house.
He knew what he had to do.

He called his Uncle Bike,
Who said he'd be right there.
"I've failed you," said young Trike.
"I'm *not* a delivery bear!"

"Fiddle-dee-sticks," said Bicycle Bear.
"We'll do what must be done.
You know," he added thoughtfully,
"Two heads are better than one."

So Trike went to the station
To meet his uncle's train.
With two bears on the job,
The answer was soon plain.

"We will move this mouse's house.
We'll deliver it with ease.
All we need," said Bicycle Bear...

"...Is a great big pair of skis!"

They set off down the hill
Through the snow and ice.
They delivered that big house
And ninety-nine small mice!

"I have ruined your vacation.
I'm sorry," said Tricycle Bear.
But his uncle only laughed and said,
"I really do not care!

"I now know what I needed
Was not to sit in the sun.

"When delivering's in your blood,
Your work is what is fun.

"What I really need is help.
I could use someone like you.
Because," said Bicycle Bear,

"Five wheels are better than two!"

Notes to Grown-ups

Major Themes

Here is a quick guide to the significant themes and concepts at work in *Bicycle Bear Rides Again*:

- Working as part of a team: major tasks can be accomplished when individuals join together in a group effort.
- Volunteering to help: when an individual pitches in to help others, not only does the task get done but the individual also has a good reason to feel good about herself or himself.

Step-by-step Ideas for Reading and Talking

Here are some ideas for further give-and-take between grown-ups and children. The following topics encourage creative discussion of *Bicycle Bear Rides Again* and invite the kind of open-ended response that is consistent with many contemporary approaches to reading, including Whole Language:

- Ask your child to think of ways he or she can volunteer to be of help at home, at school, and to a friend.

- See if your child can think of examples of when it would be impossible to accomplish a task alone, such as moving a heavy piece of furniture, etc.

Games for Learning

Games and activities can stimulate young readers and listeners alike to find out more about words, numbers, and ideas. Here are more ideas for turning learning into fun:

Rhyme Time

The story of Bicycle Bear is written in appealing rhymes. Read through the story again, leaving off the final word in each rhyme. Ask your child if he or she can complete the rhyme to help you tell the story. Follow up this review with a game of Rhyme Time. Say a common one-syllable word that has many rhymes, such as the word *bear*. You and your child can then take turns thinking of a word that rhymes with bear. Continue playing until you run out of rhyming words. Then start again with a new word.

Submarine Math

The two bears teamed up to make their last delivery — a very long submarine sandwich. Create a submarine sandwich with your child, choosing from a variety of healthy ingredients. As you assemble the sandwich together, encourage your child to use math skills like counting and estimating (for example: How many slices of cheese will you need if you place them end-to-end?).

About the Author

MICHAELA MUNTEAN is the author of many popular books for children, including the original *Bicycle Bear*.

"Bicycle Bear is one of my favorite characters. As soon as I finished writing the first book about him, I knew I wanted to write another," says Ms. Muntean. "And I have lots of wonderful nieces and nephews, so I decided that Bicycle Bear should have a niece or nephew, too."

Ms. Muntean, her husband, and three dogs live in a big, old house on Long Island.

About the Artist

DOUG CUSHMAN is the illustrator of many children's books, including the original *Bicycle Bear*.

Mr. Cushman says he really enjoyed working on this new story. "Drawing that long sandwich was fun," he says, "because I never ate anything that big, and I don't think I could. If I had a sandwich that long, I would share it with a lot of friends."

Mr. Cushman lives in Connecticut. In addition to illustrating, he enjoys writing, cooking, and playing tennis.